First Kid on Mars

Written by
Kirsty Holmes

Illustrated by
Brandon Mattless

KV-510-617

My name is Laura Crusoe. In some ways, I bet I'm just like you. I live with my Mum, Sue, and my Dad, Joe. I have a blue bedroom with blue bedcovers on my bed, because blue is my favourite colour. I'm good at maths and rubbish at spelling, and I really, really love space!

First Kid on Mars

Level 9 – Gold

WALTHAM FOREST LIBRARIES

904 000 00695940

Helpful Hints for Reading at Home

The focus phonemes (units of sound) used throughout this series are in line with the order in which your child is taught at school. This offers a consistent approach to learning whether reading at home or in the classroom.

HERE ARE SOME COMMON WORDS THAT YOUR CHILD MIGHT FIND TRICKY:

water	where	would	know	thought	through	couldn't
laughed	eyes	once	we're	school	can't	our

TOP TIPS FOR HELPING YOUR CHILD TO READ:

- Encourage your child to read aloud as well as silently to themselves.
- Allow your child time to absorb the text and make comments.
- Ask simple questions about the text to assess understanding.
- Encourage your child to clarify the meaning of new vocabulary.

This book focuses on developing independence, fluency and comprehension. It is a gold level 9 book band.

WALTHAM FOREST LIBRARIES	N
904 000 00695940	
Askews & Holts	28-May-2021
JF FIR	

I do my homework, I eat my vegetables, and I love video games.
There is one big difference between you and me, though...

I don't just dream of being an astronaut one day. I already am one!

My family, the Crusoes, are the world's first – and only – family of astronauts. Our mission is to live on Mars for a year, where we will study how plants, animals and a human family can live here on the famous red planet!

We built our base down here in Cosmos Bay because the weather on Mars can be really wild. There are lightning storms and even tornadoes! This can be a bit of an issue when you want to build a house.

Some days can be pretty crazy. One morning last week, Mum came into the control pod, where Dad and I were having breakfast.

"Joe, we need to go out today," said Mum. "The tornadoes from last night have damaged the camera on the other side of Cosmos Bay."

"Laura, you stay here. Someone will need to feed all the animals," said Dad.

"You know how grumpy Bluebell and Prue get if they miss a meal!" said Mum.

I like being in charge of the animals.

Mum and Dad study what they call the 'flora and fauna' on Mars. Flora and fauna mean plants and animals. They are trying to find out which ones will do well here. This means we have a lot of animals at the base with us.

All the animals were chosen because they can live in tough places on Earth. This means we have some strange animals here! First, I feed the dingoes. They like it when I scratch behind their ears and stroke their backs.

Then I feed our buffalo, Bluebell and Prue.
They are sisters. They have loads of shaggy,
auburn fur and they like it when I brush it.
They like to eat grass and the leaves from the
tomatoes that Dad grows.

I always save the geckoes for last because they are my favourites. There are six of them. They are so pretty, with their bright colours. The blue one always comes right up to me when he sees me. I think he likes me.

That day, after I
fed all the animals,
I went up to the
control pod to
finish my breakfast.
I pressed the button
to activate the
automatic locks and
sat down at the main desk.

But I didn't notice that one of the geckoes had
snuck out with me!

Scared, it launched
itself out of my
pocket! I tried to
catch it, but I
knocked my hot
chocolate onto
the controls! I
grabbed some
tissues and
mopped up the
liquid, but the

controls fizzed and crackled!

Uh-oh. This was going to be an issue...

The liquid had caused the automatic locks to open... and the animals had all escaped!

I had to get them all safely back into their pods before Mum and Dad got back!

I picked up the gecko. It was the little blue one! "Right, you," I said. "You caused this, so you are going to help me sort it out. But first, you need a name. How about... GALAXY!"

Galaxy smiled. I think he liked his new name. Now then, where could all the animals have gone?

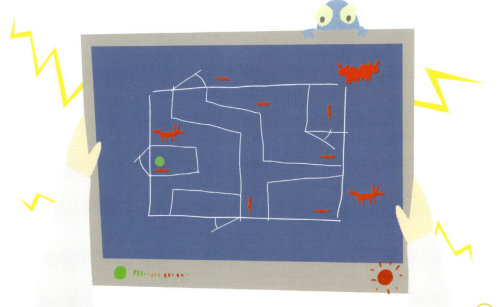

"Right, Galaxy. First, we'd better find those buffalo!" I said, popping him into my pocket. Now, I had never seen Bluebell or Prue move any faster than a lazy saunter, so they couldn't have gone far.
Just then, there was a crash from the storeroom pod.
I rushed in. There was mess everywhere!
"Oh dear," I said, with a rueful smile. The two buffaloes were mooing at me sadly.

On the floor next to them was an empty can of space glue! Somehow, they must have sat in it, and then got stuck together. Bluebell and Prue had so much space glue in their long auburn fur that they were completely stuck together!

There was nothing for it. Nothing in the world was as sticky as space glue! I grabbed a pair of shears and began to snip their auburn fur away. True, they both had giant bald patches on their haunches, but they were free!

I took them back to their pod and closed the door. Next, it was time to find the dingoes.

Galaxy stuck his head out of my pocket as if he was listening to something.

Sure enough, there was a faint barking sound. I followed the faint echoes of the barking. As I walked along the corridors, it got louder. I knew I was getting closer. Galaxy ducked into my pocket again. We were outside the laundry pod. I could hear the dingoes louder than ever...

Inside the laundry pod, the washing machines were on, washing our spare spacesuits. The dingoes were watching them go round and round, like an audience watching a sports match. Silly dingoes!

I quietly tied lots of space boots together. Then I ran down the corridor, boots rattling. Just like dogs back on Earth, the dingoes couldn't resist, and chased me all the way to their pod!
Galaxy applauded. I think he was impressed by my trick!

"OK, Galaxy. Where did all your friends go, then?" I said. Galaxy launched himself out of my pocket and ran down to the kitchen pod. It was a complete mess.

The geckoes had been here alright. It looked as though the tornadoes from outside had got in and had a party in the kitchen!
Galaxy was jumping around near a puddle of tomato sauce.
"Well done, Galaxy!" I said. "We can follow the footprints!"

Galaxy and I tracked the geckoes down the corridor. There were little sticky, saucy footprints everywhere! We whooshed through the automatic doors one by one, until finally the sauce ran out.
"Where did they go, Galaxy?" I asked.

Just then, there was a huge crash from the music pod. Poor little Galaxy launched himself at me in fright. I put him safely in my pocket. Could tiny little geckoes be making that much noise?

Sure enough, they were. Two were bouncing on the bongos. Another was twanging the taut, metallic strings of an electric guitar and one was playing with a flute!

Galaxy made one, so that was two, three, four, five...

Where was the sixth? The little red one with yellow toes?

Squeak!

There was a strange sound. I couldn't see what was causing it.

Squeak!

Just then, I caught sight of the trumpet out of the corner of my eye. There was a red tail sticking out of it!

There was only one thing for it. I lifted the trumpet and blew. All the other geckoes watched... But nothing. I blew again. "Here goes nothing!" I said. I blew again. HARD.

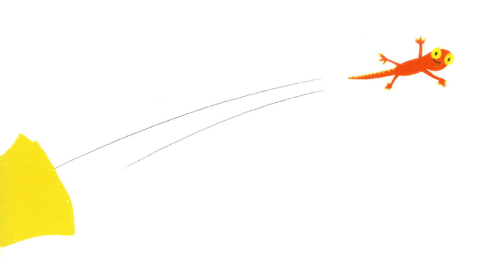

The gecko shot out of the trumpet and flew across the room! I scooped up all six geckoes and put them into my pockets. Then I made sure they were safely back in their pod and sealed the door with the last of the space glue.

I whooshed through the automatic door.
I paused by the exit to the main pod. Was
there something wriggling about in my pocket?

It was Galaxy!

"How did you get out?" I tickled his little
belly. "Well, you might as well come with me
for the morning then."
I popped Galaxy back in my pocket. I would
have to put the boots back in the laundry

pod and clean all the spilled sauce from the kitchen. It was going to be a busy morning while I waited for Mum and Dad to get back.

I shared a muffin with Galaxy and we cleaned up the desk. Mum would know how to fix the automatic locks when she got back. Until then, the space glue should hold everything.
But just then, the screen crackled into life.

"Laura? It's Mum and Dad! We got the cameras fixed. Is everything OK?" called Mum.
"Hi, Mum. Yes, everything's fine. Just a couple of small issues but nothing Galaxy and I couldn't solve," I said, winking at Galaxy.

First Kid on Mars

1. What was the Crusoe's family mission?

2. Which animals did Laura feed first?

3. How did Bluebell and Prue get stuck together?

4. What was the puddle of sauce on the kitchen floor?

   (a) Chocolate

   (b) Tomato

   (c) Cheese

5. Do you think Laura was right to hide the animal escapes from her Mum and Dad? Would you have done the same?

©2020 **BookLife Publishing Ltd.**
King's Lynn, Norfolk PE30 4LS

ISBN 978-1-83927-015-4

All rights reserved. Printed in Malaysia.
A catalogue record for this book is available from
the British Library.

First Kid on Mars
Written by Kirsty Holmes
Illustrated by Brandon Mattless

An Introduction to BookLife Readers...

Our Readers have been specifically created in line with the London Institute of Education's approach to book banding and are phonetically decodable and ordered to support each phase of the Letters and Sounds document.

Each book has been created to provide the best possible reading and learning experience. Our aim is to share our love of books with children, providing both emerging readers and prolific page-turners with beautiful books that are guaranteed to provoke interest and learning, regardless of ability.

BOOK BAND GRADED using the Institute of Education's approach to levelling.

PHONETICALLY DECODABLE supporting each phase of Letters and Sounds.

EXERCISES AND QUESTIONS to offer reinforcement and to ascertain comprehension.

BEAUTIFULLY ILLUSTRATED to inspire and provoke engagement, providing a variety of styles for the reader to enjoy whilst reading through the series.

AUTHOR INSIGHT:
KIRSTY HOLMES

Kirsty Holmes, holder of a BA, PGCE, and an MA, was born in Norfolk, England. She has written over 60 books for BookLife Publishing, and her stories are full of imagination, creativity and fun.

This book focuses on developing independence, fluency and comprehension. It is a gold level 9 book band.